A River
in Egypt

D0512858

Faber
Stories

David Means's second collection of stories, *Assorted Fire Events*, earned the *Los Angeles Times* Book Prize for fiction, and his third, *The Secret Goldfish*, was shortlisted for the Frank O'Connor International Short Story Prize. His fourth, *The Spot*, was selected as a 2010 Notable Book by the *New York Times*. His first novel, *Hystopia*, was longlisted for the Man Booker Prize. His most recent collection of short stories, *Instructions for a Funeral*, was published by Faber in 2019. Means's fiction has appeared in *The New Yorker*, *Harper's*, and *Esquire* among other publications. He lives in Nyack, New York, and teaches at Vassar College.

David
Means

A River
in Egypt

Faber
Stories

First published in this single edition in 2019
by Faber & Faber Limited
Bloomsbury House
74–77 Great Russell Street
London WC1B 3DA
First published in *The Spot* in 2010

Typeset by Faber & Faber Limited
Printed and bound by CPI Group (UK) Ltd, Croydon, CR0 4YY

A CIP record for this book
is available from the British Library

ISBN 978–0–571–35249–4

10 9 8 7 6 5 4 3 2 1

The hot air in the sweat chamber—as the nurse had called it, ushering them in—was humidified to make it even more uncomfortable, and when he loosened his tie he was reminded that he was the type who felt it necessary to dress up for hospital visits, and for air flights, not so much because he had a residual primness left over from his Midwestern upbringing, which he did, but because he felt that he might receive more attentive service if he came dressed with a certain formality, so that the nurses and doctors tending his son might see him, Cavanaugh, as a big-shot banker instead of an assistant art director who was known, if he was known at all, for his last-minute design fixes. For example, he had once turned the interior of a hotel lobby—one of the last of the classic (now defunct) SROs in midtown, the Abe Lincoln, just off Twenty-eighth and Madison—into a Victorian salon by throwing a few bolts of velvet around the windows of the downstairs smoking lobby.

Just that morning, as he was leaving for the hospital, the director, Harrison, had called to let him know that he was being dropped from *Draconian,* a big-budget sci-fi production that included a huge political convention scene, filmed in an old dirigible hangar out on Long Island—a design job that had drawn upon his expertise in plastic sheeting, banners preprinted with mock structural details, and so forth. "It's not that we don't like your work," Harrison had said. "You've got fine, visionary abilities. You see things others miss. But maybe you see too much. The problem with your design was—and I don't know how to put this—it was too real, too clear. You know where I'm coming from? One wrong move cinematographically and you're lost in the future, or lodged too far in the past. We made one wrong move, and I don't want to make another. I'm not casting blame. I'm apportioning fault. If I don't do it, the audience will. You see, my hope is to keep the film, for all its futuristic overtones, closely rooted in the present moment, and that way, as I see it, the audience will feel connected to *contemporary experience* in a way that will allow the obvious *eternal* elements"—Harrison was apparently referring to the assassination attempt, and to the corrupt, smooth-talking monomaniacal presidential candidate who was secretly implanting electronic doohickeys into his opponents' temples in order to create a network of paranoid, deranged sapsouls, as he put it—"to resonate fully not

3

only with current audiences but also with future audiences. So the trick to fostering believability lies in tweaking the extremely fine fissure between the known present and the unknowable future. If it's tweaked correctly, even years from now an audience will ignore the errors and focus only on the viable world that had once really existed, and still exists, in all human interaction."

Cavanaugh pondered all of the above—along with images from the drive that morning over the Tappan Zee Bridge and the beauty the river had held, stretching toward Tarrytown, rippled with tight wavelets, shimmering blue under a pristine sky—as he held his son, Gunner, in the sweat chamber, talked to him, got him settled, and gave him his toys, extracting them one at a time from an old green rucksack. These toys had been put aside for a few days so that they might accrue some elemental newness again and, in turn, give more in the way of pleasure. ("There are enough old toys to keep him busy," Sharon had insisted. "I can't charge another toy on the card, and I think we should build up his desire so that when Christmas comes there's not another huge letdown like there was last year. Case in point: You bought him that Gobberblaster gun last summer, which was totally inappropriate for a kid his age and might've been a perfect gift for Christmas a couple of years from now, and he went out and shot it a few times, and now it's in the back of the closet like all his other junked toys.")

That fight about buying Gunner some new toys for the test, he thought, dabbing the sweat from his brow onto his cuff, had really been spurred on by the fact that Sharon was now back in practice, commuting into the city to scrounge clients and taking on a disproportionate number of pro bono cases, as if to keep the financial burden firmly on his side of the ledger, because she felt—and he knew this from their ten years together—that pressure was good for him artistically, and that he'd find the strength to break through to the big time only if he pushed against the weight of their monetary need. So he extracted one toy at a time and watched as Gunner went to the floor, tinkered and fussed and depleted each quickly, and in less than ten minutes had already gone through the Emergency Tow Truck and something called the Question Cube after two lame questions:

*What river is in Egypt? the Nile? the
Hudson? the Thames? or the Kalamazoo?*

And then:

*Who said: Sometimes a cigar is just
a cigar? Groucho Marx? William
Shakespeare? Sigmund Freud? or King
Edward?*

before the Question Cube gave a weak static
snort and faded into silence, so that little
Gunner, who was really too young to know the
correct answers, but who liked the sound of
the toy's artificial voice—a basso profundo—
and got a thrill out of guessing, stood up and,
with a grunt, gave it a hard kick. Then he went
on to quickly sap the Zinger, a gravity-defying
top that was said to have the ability—in correct

conditions—to spin eternally, and his old favorite, Mad Hamlet, a strangely compelling action figure that went into suicidal fits when you pushed a button hidden on its back. Only ten minutes in the sweat chamber had gone by, and all Cavanaugh could do was wait a few beats while Gunner looked up, bright with anticipation, and then cried, "I'm hot, I'm hot, I'm hot, hot, hot."

At this point, stalling for time, Cavanaugh put the rucksack out of sight behind his back and waited a few more beats before pulling it out again, saying, "Hey, hey, look, another rucksack," and shook it near the boy's head until he stopped flailing around, looked up with his ruddy face (the kid had what the doctor called dermagraphic skin—highly sensitive, prone to rashes), and said, "Give me, give me." At which point Cavanaugh unzipped the rucksack slowly and said, "Let's pretend it's Christmas morning and we're just up, having had our traditional morning cocoa and sweet roll"—Christmas was the one morning each year that they opened up the tightly packed dough, popping it against the counter and rolling out the spiral of cardboard foil—"and now Santa's bringing some new presents," and then, with great flourish, saying, "Ta da," he reached in and pulled out the Emergency Tow Truck again, squat and malformed, with a thick front bumper, holding it out and watching as Gunner's face composed itself around a cry, restrained itself for a second, his tiny mouth a tight rictus of pink next to which his cheeks bunched to reveal a remnant of his original baby face—womb wet with sweat, blue with blood, and dramatically horrific. Cavanaugh searched the boy's

9

face the way a sailor might read the twilight sky, and saw clearly that he was about to unfurl a squall-cry, a true record breaker on the scream scale. And he did. When it came, it was a squawking, ducklike sound, odd in its guttural overtones, yet paradoxically bright, shiny, and thin, like a drawn thread of hot glass. This was a cry that said: You led me to believe, fully and completely, that I was about to receive a newborn toy, something that would match my deepest expectations. This was a cry that rent open the universe and, in doing so, peeled back and exposed some soft, vulnerable tissue in Cavanaugh's brain.

So that what he did next was, he thought later, simply an act of self-protection, reaching out and yanking the boy onto his feet and into one arm and then, with the cup of his hand, sealing the kid's mouth shut, so that all Cavanaugh felt was the small, frail puffs against his palm as he spoke down into the hot, sweaty bloom of struggling face, saying, "Jesus Christ, Daddy was just playing a game, a Christmas game. Daddy was just trying to lighten the situation and keep you from doing what you're doing right now. Daddy just wants his Gunner to behave himself, if not for the sake of the nurses—who, I'm sure, are out in the hall about to bust in here to see what's going on—then for Daddy himself, who is at his wits' end and wants this test to go as smoothly as possible." At which point, as if on cue, the door opened, bringing in fresh air that smelled of disinfectant and hospital floor polish, and a nurse, beautiful in her tight uniform, with long blond hair, who said, "Oh, dear," and presented a face, he later thought, that was readable in an infinite number of ways—soft around the mouth, with a wry smile that just about verged on a frown, set in a snowy Nordic topography of bone structure. From the nose down, she seemed to be frank and nonjudgmental, her mouth loose around unavailable words; from the nose up, her two intensely blue eyes and a single raised eyebrow seemed to be saying: Something funny's going on here. Something's not right. Something's deeply wrong about the way you're cupping the boy's mouth in relation to the way he (the boy) is standing, in relation to the way you are looming behind him, in relation to the sheen of his terrified face, in relation to that cry I heard out in the hallway, which was so loud and shrill it penetrated the door and reached my ears. And then she tilted her face slightly to one side, glanced at the room (really nothing but two chairs and a heating unit lit with stark neon), and made a face that seemed to admit: Maybe for you, as a father, this is a trying test, though it's certainly nothing compared with a bone-marrow biopsy, a spinal tap, or the claustrophobia of the MRI ring. But, yes (her face seemed to say), the analysis of the sweat in order to rule out, or to rule in, cystic fibrosis makes it oracular in nature, and in a few hours you, sir, will be offered up the results, and said results might give you a positive yes on the disease, which would mean, of course, that Gunner will face a future of hard breathing, clotted phlegm, and, most certainly, a relatively early death (in his thirties, if you're lucky), but all this in no way excuses you, sir, from what appeared to be transpiring when I passed the door and heard the cries and stepped in to take a look.

In response to what he seemed to be seeing in her facial expressions, Cavanaugh said, "We're fine, just a little misunderstanding about the toy bag, the rucksack here, regarding Christmas, pretending it's Christmas, trying to keep him calm. I mean to say," he said, as he fingered the dimple on his tie, "I was trying to recharge these toys, so to speak, to make them surprising again, you know, and Gunner became disappointed and began to cry. Not that crying isn't normal in these circumstances."

Something stony seemed to enter the nurse's features as she listened, taking another step into the room, nodding slightly, looking down at the boy and then up at Cavanaugh. Did her eyes narrow slightly? Was there a shift, barely perceptible, in the set of her teeth? Did some interrogative element enter her eyes, brightening the corneas? It seemed to him that she was thinking: We clearly have a situation here. To cup a boy's mouth like that is wrong, sinful, actually, and just a precursor to more violent acts; God knows what's going on behind closed doors. And it seemed to him that her face (and the way she moved up to Gunner and touched his head lightly, patting him, and then moved to adjust the collecting device) also said: I've seen a thousand such moments, entering rooms to witness patients adjusting their postures, ashamed, awkward around the impersonal equipment, awaiting test results that may change their future. I've entered rooms to find patients yanking out IV needles. I've opened the door to scenes of fornication, to

15

urine-stained old men with pocked behinds. I've opened doors to couples enfolded in weeping embraces, so seized with grief that they had to be pried apart. I've opened doors to bald-headed children with angelic eyes and shattering smiles. But this is different because of the cry itself—the desperation and the tonal quality in relation (again) to your unusually guilty face, in relation (once again) to the boy's self-protective, conspiratorial slack expression, as if he were hiding something, in relation (once again) to the position of the hand held over the mouth, in relation to the finger marks on the flesh around the mouth. Then her lips tightened and her cheekbones—yes, cheekbones!— seemed to sharpen, and her face seemed to say to Cavanaugh: I might have to report this to the resident social worker, just as a matter of protocol. Not because I'm absolutely certain that you struck the child but because I'm *not certain,* and if I don't do it and further harm comes to this boy I'll never forgive myself and I'll sit forever down in my own particular hell.

Then the nurse said, "Oh, you poor little boy. We're a long way off from Christmas. But we're not a long way off from finishing the test. You're a brave boy. A brave, brave boy."

Woe to the man whose child is on the verge of a diagnosis, her face then seemed to say as she ran her fingers along the tape, removed the electrode wires, cleaned Gunner's arm with a gauze pad, secured the collecting device, checked the tubing, and then, without another word, heaved out of the chamber, latched the door, tested the seal, and glanced back through the oval window with a face that said: I understand that your game with the toys in the bag was creative and a sign that you're a good father, if somewhat desperate, and then she was gone and he turned to Gunner and said, "Daddy got in trouble because you were crying. Daddy got scolded, not verbally, but facially, so let's pretend again, and do the Christmas grab bag, but do it right this time and really pretend I'm Santa." And he opened the bag and pulled out his trump card, a toy he had left out in the first rotation, one of Gunner's all-time favorites, Weird Willy the Spasmodic Doll. When switched on, Weird Willy flexed and yawed spastically, like an injured athlete, and performed a ballet of crude movements while his internal mechanisms poked and prodded through his rubbery skin. The toy, seemingly crucified from within, proved agonizing to watch. Not long ago, back in August, Weird Willy had provided a full afternoon of entertainment in a patch of sunlight beneath the dining room table. Gunner and Willy had spent a good hour conversing, Gunner saying softly, "Stop that, you stupid freak, you pathetic idiot, you stupid stupid." Now, in the sweat chamber, Weird Willy said, "Haa wee, haa wee," while Gunner said, "Die, die, die," and wrung Willy's torso with both hands, trying his best to tear him limb from limb.

"And that was the end of Weird Willy, the end of the toys, and the end of my Christmas morning scheme, as I think of it now," Cavanaugh muttered to himself as he started home from the hospital, barely moving his lips over the words, imagining what he might say to his shrink, Dr. Brackett, at his next appointment. In the rearview mirror, Gunner, strapped into his safety seat, gave him a suspicious frown. Cavanaugh closed his lips and imagined saying, "When I'm with him, I'm always aware of the value timewise. I mean, in terms of using up time, of entertainment value, so to speak, of whatever catches his attention. Even when I'm not with him. For example, just a few months ago I was on location in California, working on *Draconian,* and I was driving up the Pacific Coast Highway, trying to solve a design problem. President Gleason, after his big defeat, goes off on his own for a few weeks to a cabin near Big Sur to ponder his past and begin writing his memoirs, because he sees himself—according to the script—as part of a great lineage of memoir writers stretching back to Ulysses S. Grant and, strangely, up to Jack Kerouac.

"Anyway, I envisioned the scene as a biblical moment that mirrored Jesus' desert solitude. Something had to point away from the stereotypical writer gestures (Gleason leaning morosely over his laptop keyboard; Gleason flipping his pencil between his fingers, biting his lip, pacing the room; Gleason pouring himself a huge glass of Scotch and swirling it gently before he takes a drink) and direct the audience subtly to the deeper perplexities of his crestfallen state. So I designed chinks in the cabin's mortar that, when lit from behind, shot small beams—or maybe you'd call them shafts—of light through the walls and the dust motes, forming crosses through which he might walk during one of his pacing-for-inspiration scenes.

"In any case, I was driving up the coast, thinking about this problem, when I became acutely aware of the vista—the hard, purging waves roiling in, the whitecaps foaming far out, and the milky blue of the water—and it suddenly occurred to me that I could, with great precision, calculate the exact amount of time that Gunner would, if prompted (*Hey, Gunner, take a look at that*), examine each scene before turning away. I could decipher —is that the word?—the exact amount of entertainment value specific scenes on the coast would offer my boy. Waves slamming around hard, bountiful rocks, breaking in a dramatic foam, no matter how fantastically beautiful, would distract him for twenty-eight seconds. Sea lions—if we walked down to get a close look—would tap out at three minutes of distraction value. A frigate, viewed through a pair of field glasses? Five minutes and thirty seconds. A supertanker, not too far from shore, but in heavy surf on the edge of trouble? Six good, solid minutes. (The field glasses would have to be new and never used before.) A frigate on fire? Seven, or possibly eight, minutes of attention. A supertanker engulfed in a raging inferno, belching a thick plume of fire? Nine. A sinking ship (with attendant oil spill and terror-stricken passengers waving frantically, some of them dashing across the deck, on fire)? Ten minutes. Albeit none of these calculations, no matter how accurate they might have felt, were really precise, because one had to go plus or minus twenty seconds on one side or the other to account for

various other distractions (fiddling, scratch-
ing, eye rubbing, and snot blowing) that might
cut into his attention span.

"So you see, to get to the point, when I
handed him Weird Willy I had the toy figured
at less than a minute. What does any of it matter, his crying, so long as he sweats enough
to fill the fucking testing device, I should've
thought. I should've thought, I'm lucky that
my son is just crying and not spazzing out, or
giving me a much harder time. I'm lucky that
he's only being tested for this disease and
hasn't been handed a diagnosis: terminally
ill, with only a few weeks, or a day, or even
less, to live, for sure, and that this is still a
wide-open thing," he would tell Dr. Brackett,
at his office in White Plains.

Outside, down in the street, the traffic
signals would be cheeping, making a sound

meant to guide the blind, if there were any. In the four years that he'd been going over the bridge to visit Dr. Brackett, he had never seen a single blind soul using the audible signals to cross the street. The streets in White Plains were always dusty and forlorn, and somehow reminded him of a Western town just before a shootout; folks were hidden away, peeking out in anticipation of violence. Even up in the office he'd feel this—while hearing the cheeping sounds—and it would form a backdrop as Dr. Brackett, a small, lean, sharp-chinned man, placed his palms on his knees and leaned forward to say something like:

"It is perfectly possible that you didn't loosen the collecting device when you grappled with your son. After all, the nurse came in and adjusted it, didn't she? You can't be blamed for that. I'm sure it happens all the time. In any case, let's focus on the wider theatrics of your parenting actions: Do you think you're the first father to cup his son around the mouth? You're a good man with a clean heart, not perfectly clean but clear (yes, a clear heart), and you had good intentions, and you were just at the end of your rope, and so you naturally felt frustrated and fearful—above all fearful, because what the test meant, most certainly, one way or another, was the central element/key/crux in the parental drama (let's call it a drama, not a play). You were fending off, or, rather, delaying for as long as possible, the end result of the test, perhaps subconsciously. You were biding your time with Gunner, trying to fend off, if I may use that phrase again, his anxiety, or what you imagined was his anxiety, by inducing play, a certain level of play, presumably, not just using up time or trying to keep him calm, as you claim, but trying to keep the scene itself stable and quiet on some level, maybe thinking, as you tried, that in doing so you'd also somehow, and perhaps this is a long shot"— he would admit, because Dr. Brackett, as a shrink, liked to counter and undercut his own statements as a way of enlivening them, making them seem like organic, natural formations in order to assure his patient that he was just as human as the next guy and didn't subscribe to the old formalities of Freudian methodology—"but perhaps you were also under the belief that, somehow, if you kept Gunner quiet and calm, the outcome of the test might be positively affected. Because you believed, I believe, that there were, and are, deeper factors at play—quantum/God/ mystical, take your pick—and that if the test went smoothly the results were more likely to be negative. You felt, at that moment, in the sweat chamber, after the toys gave out, a sense that in the heat of the room, and in the sweat that was being exuded from Gunner's body, fate was at hand, so to speak." (Here Brackett would draw a couple of deep breaths.) "Now that you know that the results of that particular test were inconclusive because the collection device came loose and, in the end, not enough sweat was collected, you blame yourself for the fact that you've got to go back next week and again reopen that door to the question of his health, and that in doing so you must once again face the possibility that he has cystic fibrosis, and that your life will change again," Brackett would say.

"Now let's backtrack a little. The nurse, who presumably has been through many of these moments with many other patients, most likely came into the so-called sweat chamber to offer assistance, to help you in one way or another, or to remove the electrodes, and in seeing your hand over Gunner's mouth she understood your predicament and sympathized with it and with the boy's predicament, too—perhaps your own more so than the boy's—and at that moment she did not judge you as harshly as you'd like to think, but was actually waiting for you to speak, and in hearing your anger, when you did speak, and within it your deep, almost Jobian fear, felt her own helplessness before all the illness she has faced, as you were saying. Bald cancer heads, forlorn eyes, tears, kids suffering at the deepest level. Kids cheery and chipper against the saddest odds.

Kids with that disjointed misunderstanding of their own place and status, not only healthwise but otherwise, too. Kids bucking themselves up heroically. Clearly, just going by the fact that you continue to mention what her Mona Lisa face seemed to be saying, almost obsessively, it seems to me, it becomes evident that you were turning to her as a soothsayer, and maybe that might mean, and here I propose this only as a theory, a useful one—perhaps, perhaps not—that she, too, felt herself to be unwillingly put into a shamanic position; no, let's correct that and say an oracular mode. Let's say she felt that her face might—from your point of view—be seen as an oracle, and let's say that that might explain the strange expressions she presented, if they really were strange."

———

Cavanaugh imagined all of the above as he drove back over the Hudson while Gunner slept in the backseat with his head lolling to one side and his tiny mouth open around his own breath, and, down below, the river fretted with bits of white chop as the first hard wind of the fall drove down from the north and cut past Hook Mountain on its way to the city. As he drove, he began to cry, openly and with stifled guffaws, the way a man must cry when he is faced with the future, any future, a good one or a bad one, and after he has sat alone in a room with his child, waiting for sweat to collect so that he may know something about what is to come, some exactitude in the form of a diagnosis; he cried the way a man must cry when he's driving, keeping both hands on the wheel and his eyes wide open through the blur, and he cried the way a man must cry when he is exhausted from being up deep into the night while his boy coughs up almost unbelievable quantities of phlegm, clearly succumbing to a disease process—as his doctor called it—that at that point was indeterminate; he cried for himself as much as for his son, and for the world that was unfolding to his left, an open vista, the gaping mouth of the river, which at that moment was flowing down to the sea, hurrying itself into the heart of New York Harbor. He was crying like a man on a bridge—suspended between two sides of life, trapped in the blunt symbolism of the spans, and atop the floating pylons that sustained the decks of reinforced concrete—while his son slept soundly, unburdened now, it seemed, when Cavanaugh looked back at him in the mirror, and afloat on his own slumber. Not at all sick, or diseased, and free from whatever torment the future might offer up. By the time (three minutes later) that Cavanaugh was exiting off the thruway and driving down Main Street (six minutes later), past the stately trees unfurling their fall brilliance, he had collected himself and was clear-eyed and in a new state. He wasn't a man reborn at all. Not even close. That would come much later, after the second test, and when the results were in, conclusive and hard, no nonsense in the statement they made. That would come (he imagined) when he gave himself over to the fact that salt moved chaotically in and out of certain cells, and that Gunner's body would forever confront certain facts: mucous blockages in his lungs and pancreas, and frequent infections. But for now, as he entered the town on a beautiful fall day, the diagnosis was somewhere off in the remote future, and he was alive and dealing with the moment at hand, which included his own actions in the sweat room, and the failure of his set design for the convention scene, and he felt himself growing calm before the sweet presence in the backseat, which came to him in the form of a soft snore, a little clicking sound that accompanied each exhalation, and then, finally, a small groan as the car settled over the curb of the driveway (eight minutes later) and came to a stop, and then another slight sniff as his boy awoke (one minute later), roused by the silence, the lack of road noise, and opened his eyes and blinked, and then said, "Are we home? Are we home now, Dad?"